ANDY TELLS THE TRUTH

SEEDLiNGS

BOOKS TO GROW ON

Chariot Books™
David C. Cook Publishing Co.

Andy Tells the Truth gives you an opportunity to talk with your children about honesty. To get the discussion started, use these questions: When is it hard for you to be honest? What helped Andy to keep from cheating? What can help you when you're tempted to cheat? Why was Jesus happy that Andy didn't cheat?

Chariot Books™ is an imprint of David C. Cook Publishing Co.
David C. Cook Publishing Co., Elgin, Illinois 60120
David C. Cook Publishing Co., Weston, Ontario
Nova Distribution Ltd., Newton Abbot, England

ANDY TELLS THE TRUTH

Written by Terry Thornton
Illustrated by Bartholomew
Cover designed by Helen Lannis
First Printing Revised Edition, 1994
Printed in the United States of America
98 97 96 95 94   5 4 3 2 1
ISBN 0-7814-1537-3

Originally titled *How Many Jawbreakers?*

Someone would win the jar of
jawbreakers on Mrs. Allen's desk.
I hoped it would be me, Andy Jackson.

Whoever guessed how many jawbreakers were in the jar would win. Mrs. Allen said we would write down our answers this afternoon.

After lunch we went outside to play. Mrs. Allen asked me to go get her whistle. When I found it, right next to it was a note that said, "732 jawbreakers." It was the answer to the contest!

I took the whistle back to Mrs. Allen. During the kickball game I couldn't stop thinking about those jawbreakers!

Then I thought of something else. To write "732" on my paper would be cheating. "Jesus," I prayed, "help me do what's right."

After the game, Mrs. Allen asked, "Did anyone see a piece of paper that was here on my desk?"

It was hard, but I said, "Yes, Mrs. Allen. I saw it, but I won't guess that number. I will guess something else."

Mrs. Allen said, "Thank you, Andy. I'm glad you are honest. Everyone write down your answers and pass them up."
I wrote down 237.
It felt good to do the right thing!
I know Jesus was happy too.

At last, Mrs. Allen said, "I'm very happy that Andy told the truth. That number on my desk was Christy's guess. She had to leave early today and left it there."
I was glad I hadn't cheated. 732 might not be the right answer after all!

Mrs. Allen said, "There were 232 jawbreakers. The winner is Andy Jackson. Congratulations, Andy! How did you think of 237?"

"It was an honest guess, Mrs. Allen.
A real honest guess."

"A good man is known by his truthfulness;
a false man by deceit and lies."

Proverbs 12:17 Taken from *The Illustrated Bible* (TLB)

Jesus wants us always to tell the truth and not cheat. What would you have done if you were Andy?

SEEDLiNGS

BOOKS TO GROW ON